I AM WHO I SEE I AM!

ADRIANA CLARK-RAMBERT

ISBN 978-1-64258-806-4 (hardcover)
ISBN 978-1-64258-805-7 (digital)

Christian Faith Publishing, Inc.
832 Park Avenue
Meadville, PA 16335
www.christianfaithpublishing.com

Printed in the United States of America

WHO IS GODISS LOVE?

She is a voice. Comfortable to speak her mind. She's trying to build herself up. Her goals involve adding value to other people's lives because she is a woman of passion. She's kind, she's tough, but don't take her for granted. Nobody is built like her. Her goal is to exude love and give it to every human she touches. She's fragile, but she's a rock. Recognize her ability quickly because she is the total package. She is that ready, and if not, we will make her so!

The mission is to teach our young girls and youth how to feel strong and independent. To know beauty comes from within and not from the outside. Smart is the new sexy.

Our job is to protect the rights of young people. To fight for these rights. To speak for those who have no voice of their own.

Godiss Love is dedicated to serving all God's children with absolute respect and unconditional love. Anything you want or desire in your life, you already have the power to achieve it. With the inspirational messages from this book, you will have the power right now to control how you think, how you feel, and how you become the best version of you. Praying, putting God first, and loving yourself are three simple keys to happiness. Love is God. God is love!

GOD iss Love

ABOVE ALL THINGS . . .
GOD REMAINS FIRST!

COINCIDENCE IS GOD'S WAY
OF STAYING ANONYMOUS.
THERE ARE NO ACCIDENTS.
GOD IS A POWERFUL GOD.

*BE THE BEST
VERSION OF YOU.*

3

IF YOU NOTICE A NEGATIVE
THOUGHT STARTING TO
CREEP IN, CONFRONT IT
WITH A POSITIVE ONE. YOU
WILL BE ABLE TO CONQUER
NEGATIVE THINKING IF
YOU KEEP DOING THIS.

GREATNESS IS DETERMINED BY YOUR ABILITY TO BE ALL YOU CAN BE IN THE PLACE GOD HAS POSITIONED YOU.

BE STILL SO YOU DON'T MISS THE BEAUTIFUL THINGS GOD IS DOING IN YOUR LIFE.

GETTING LOST IS THE PERFECT TIME FOR DISCOVERIES.

IF YOU BELIEVE,
YOU SHALL RECEIVE!
COMMIT TO IT,
AND YOU WILL
ACHIEVE!

*BEING RUINED
IS THE ROAD TO
TRANSFORMATION.*

DON'T PASS JUDGMENT,
FOR YOU DO NOT KNOW
WHERE SOMEONE HAS BEEN
IN THEIR LIFE. YOU MAY BE
PRIVY TO THEIR SURFACE
OF CIRCUMSTANCE, BUT
YOU DON'T KNOW THE
EXTENT OF THEIR
JOURNEY.

MAY IT NOT BE
I WHO LIVES
BUT YOU, LORD,
WHO LIVES IN ME.

MAKE YOURSELF TO BE SO MUCH LIKE CHRIST THAT WHEN PEOPLE SEE YOU, THEY WILL WANT TO KNOW YOU BETTER.

YOUR TALENT IS WHAT GOD GIFTS YOU WITH. WHAT YOU DO WITH IT IS YOUR GIFT BACK TO HIM.

WHEN PEOPLE TRY TO CONDEMN YOU, PRAY FOR THEM, FOR THEY DO NOT KNOW WHAT THEY DO. FORGIVE THEM AND MOVE ON.

*SOMETIMES YOU FIND
YOURSELF WONDERING
WHY WHAT YOU ARE TRYING
TO PURSUE ISN'T QUITE
WORKING OUT. THAT'S BECAUSE
WHAT YOU MAY HAVE IN
MIND FOR YOURSELF ISN'T
WHAT GOD HAS PLANNED
FOR YOU. THANK HIM
FOR SAVING YOU!*

16

WHEN IT COMES TO YOUR CAREERS OR LIFE PATH CHOICES, PLANT YOUR SEEDS, WATER THEM WITH FOLLOW-UP, AND THEN LET THEM DO THEIR DUE DILIGENCE. IF THOSE SEEDS ARE IN HIS PLAN FOR YOU, THEY WILL GROW INTO SOMETHING BEAUTIFUL OR WITHER AND FADE.

BEGIN NOW
LIVING YOUR LIFE,
MOMENT BY MOMENT,
KNOWING GOD IS
IN YOU.

LEARN TO TRUST GOD. REMEMBER HE IS SMARTER THAN YOU, SO BE WILLING TO DO WHAT HE SAYS, WHETHER IT MAKES SENSE TO YOU OR NOT. OBEY EVEN HIS SMALLEST INSTRUCTION. IF YOU DO, HE WILL EVENTUALLY CHANGE YOUR WHOLE LIFE . . . ONE STEP AT A TIME.

IF YOU WANT TO HEAR FROM GOD, YOU WILL HAVE TO SET ASIDE YOUR OWN AMBITIONS AND DESIRES. SPEND TIME IN PRAYER AND IN THE WORD. TUNE YOUR EAR TO THE VOICE OF THE SPIRIT—HIS SPIRIT.

THE TRUTH IS YOU PROBABLY ALREADY KNOW ONE THING GOD WANTS YOU TO CHANGE OR DO. YOU MIGHT NOT KNOW WHY HE WANTS YOU TO DO IT, YOU MIGHT NOT KNOW WHERE IT'S LEADING, BUT YOU'VE HEARD THIS VOICE IN YOUR HEART. FOLLOW IT.

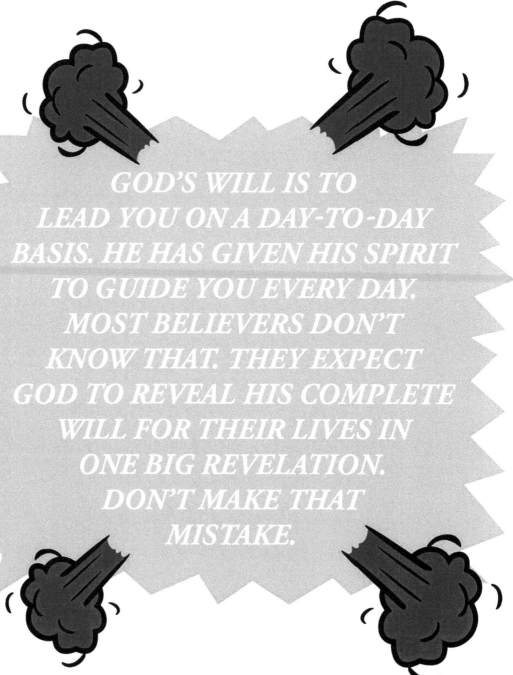

GOD'S WILL IS TO
LEAD YOU ON A DAY-TO-DAY
BASIS. HE HAS GIVEN HIS SPIRIT
TO GUIDE YOU EVERY DAY.
MOST BELIEVERS DON'T
KNOW THAT. THEY EXPECT
GOD TO REVEAL HIS COMPLETE
WILL FOR THEIR LIVES IN
ONE BIG REVELATION.
DON'T MAKE THAT
MISTAKE.

NEVER SURRENDER TO LIMITATIONS. CRISIS IS THE TIME TO BREAK BARRIERS. DO NOT BE AFRAID TO FAIL. YOU WILL NEVER SUCCEED GREATLY IF YOU ARE AFRAID TO FAIL GREATLY. BE WILLING TO TRY ANYTHING AT LEAST ONCE. IT IS BETTER TO HAVE TRIED AND FAILED THAN TO NEVER KNOW YOU COULD HAVE SUCCEEDED.

*WHAT YOU NEED IS
INSIDE YOU. YOU HAVE TO
INITIATE SOLUTIONS. DO NOT
WAIT FOR THINGS TO HAPPEN
TO YOU. TAKE CONTROL AND
DECIDE WHAT HAPPENS.
YOU HAVE TO PLACE DEMANDS
ON YOUR POTENTIAL. YOUR
ANSWERS MAY BE FOUND IN
A TALENT OR ABILITY
YOU LEAST EXPECTED.*

24

*THERE ARE WAYS
TO RISE ABOVE CRISIS.
THE GATES CANNOT PREVAIL
AGAINST YOU.*

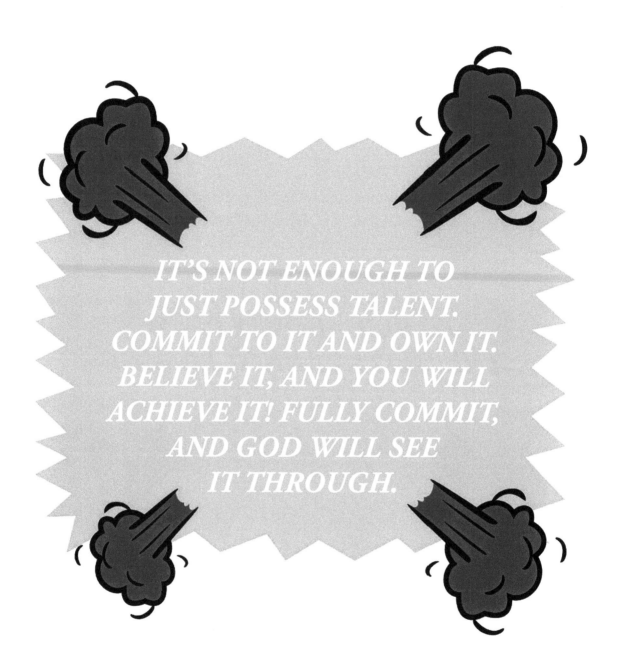

IT'S NOT ENOUGH TO
JUST POSSESS TALENT.
COMMIT TO IT AND OWN IT.
BELIEVE IT, AND YOU WILL
ACHIEVE IT! FULLY COMMIT,
AND GOD WILL SEE
IT THROUGH.

IF YOU ARE BLESSED WITH THE GIFT OF MOTHERHOOD, EMBRACE IT, FOR IT IS THE GIFT OF LIFE! CHILDREN, HONOR YOU MOTHER!

LIFE IS MOMENTS.
BE PRESENT IN EVERY
ONE OF THEM!

IN THIS LIFE, THERE IS NO SUCH THING AS A FINISH LINE. ONCE YOU ACCOMPLISH ONE DREAM, GOD WILL GIVE YOU ANOTHER. LEARN TO ENJOY THE PATH YOU ARE ON, AND DON'T RUSH TO THE END. LEARN TO ENJOY THE PEOPLE IN YOUR LIFE. LEARN TO ENJOY THE BLESSINGS OF WALKING IN THE PATH THE LORD HAS PREPARED FOR YOU.

DON'T ALLOW OTHERS TO GET THE BEST OF YOU. SILENCE IS THE BEST FORM OF REVENGE, AND PRAYER IS EVEN STRONGER! DON'T LET ANYONE STEAL YOUR JOY!

YOU CAN'T WORRY
ABOUT THINGS THAT
ARE BEYOND YOUR
CONTROL.

SEEK FIRST THE KINGDOM OF GOD, AND ALL OTHER THINGS WILL BE ADDED UNTO YOU.

DON'T JUST INVITE
GOD IN; INVOLVE HIM!

WE SOMETIMES WONDER WHY CERTAIN PEOPLE ARE PLACED IN OUR LIVES. WHEN YOU BEGIN TO UNDERSTAND GOD AND HIS WAYS, YOU WILL UNDERSTAND IT'S NOT ALWAYS ABOUT YOU. SOME PEOPLE'S ONLY ACCESS TO GOD IS THROUGH YOU.

IF YOU USE WHAT YOU HAVE, GOD WILL MAKE IT WHAT YOU NEED!

ONLY HE CAN OPEN DOORS NO MAN CAN SHUT!

GOD HAS UNIQUELY AND STRATEGICALLY PLACED YOU INTO THE PUZZLE OF THE BODY OF CHRIST. THERE WILL NEVER BE ANOTHER YOU. YOU ARE A DESIGNER'S ORIGINAL. GOD PLANNED YOU. HE MADE HIS GIFT MIX OF YOU.

TAKE A PRAYER WALK!
GOD WANTS TO SPEAK
TO YOU, BUT YOU MUST
GET TO THE PLACE TO GET
TO THE MESSAGE. GET OUT
OF YOUR CONVENIENCE!
YOU WILL ALWAYS FIND
PURPOSE IN HIS PRESENCE.
GO WHERE YOU ARE
NOT DISTRACTED.

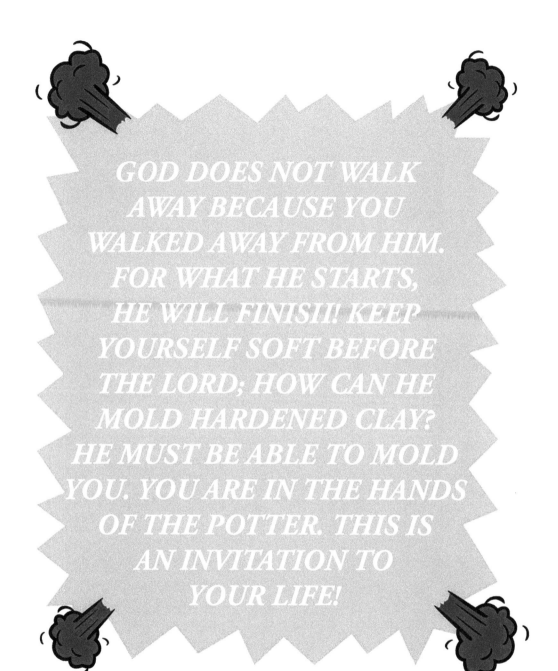

GOD DOES NOT WALK AWAY BECAUSE YOU WALKED AWAY FROM HIM. FOR WHAT HE STARTS, HE WILL FINISH! KEEP YOURSELF SOFT BEFORE THE LORD; HOW CAN HE MOLD HARDENED CLAY? HE MUST BE ABLE TO MOLD YOU. YOU ARE IN THE HANDS OF THE POTTER. THIS IS AN INVITATION TO YOUR LIFE!

JESUS IS YOUR GOD-GIVEN POTENTIAL.

DON'T LET CIRCUMSTANCE MESS UP YOUR JOY! LET JOY OVERCOME YOUR CIRCUMSTANCE.

BE SLOW TO SPEAK,
QUICK TO LISTEN,
AND SLOW TO ANGER.

ONCE YOU CAN ACCEPT HUMILITY, KNOW GOD WILL COMFORT, PROTECT, AND PROVIDE FOR YOU.

DON'T TRY AND SERVE YOUR THOUGHTS; ALWAYS SERVE GOD'S.

YOU CANNOT CHANGE PEOPLE, BUT YOU CAN CHANGE THE WAY YOU CHOOSE TO DEAL WITH THEM AND THE CIRCUMSTANCES.

*GOD WILL NEVER LEAVE
YOU NOR FORSAKE YOU.
JUST WHEN YOU THINK YOU
ARE DOWN TO NOTHING,
GOD IS ALWAYS UP
TO SOMETHING.*

ANYTHING HIDING IN THE DARK WILL COME TO LIGHT WITHOUT THE USE OF A FLASHLIGHT (METAPHORICALLY SPEAKING).

FROM THIS DAY FORWARD, ALL YOUR NEEDS ARE MET ACCORDING TO GOD'S RICHES IN GLORY BY CHRIST JESUS.

YOU ARE WAY TOO
BLESSED TO BE
STRESSED!

DELIGHT YOURSELF IN THE LORD, AND HE WILL GIVE YOU THE DESIRES OF YOUR HEART.

PEOPLE ARE
WHO THEY ARE.
DON'T STOP BEING
YOU!

*TRUST IN THE
LORD WITH ALL
YOU HEART, AND LEAN
NOT ON YOUR OWN
UNDERSTANDING. IN ALL
WAYS, ACKNOWLEDGE
HIM, AND HE WILL
MAKE YOUR PATHS
STRAIGHT.*

HAVING THE FEAR OF GOD MEANS YOU HAVE SUCH A LOVE AND REVERENCE FOR GOD THAT YOU ARE AFRAID OF WHAT LIFE WOULD BE LIKE WITHOUT HIM.

WHEN YOU COME TO A
DOUBTFUL SITUATION
IN YOUR LIFE, KNOW GOD
IS NOT THE AUTHOR
OF CONFUSION.

*WHEN YOU LET
GO AND GIVE IT TO
GOD, DO NOT TRY
AND TAKE IT BACK
FROM HIM!*

MESSAGE FROM GOD:

DO YOU THINK I WOULD HARM YOU? I DON'T PUT WEAKER PEOPLE IN YOUR LIFE TO PUNISH YOU. HOW CAN OTHERS WHO ARE WEAK GROW IF THERE IS NO STRONGER PERSON THERE TO PUSH THEM? I CREATE STRENGTH IN THOSE WHOM I KNOW CAN SUSTAIN AND FEED THE CHAIN OF LIFE. FEEL BLESSED TO HAVE THIS GIFT. EVEN THOUGH AT TIMES IT MAY FEEL CHALLENGING, IT'S ALSO TEACHING YOU AS WELL.

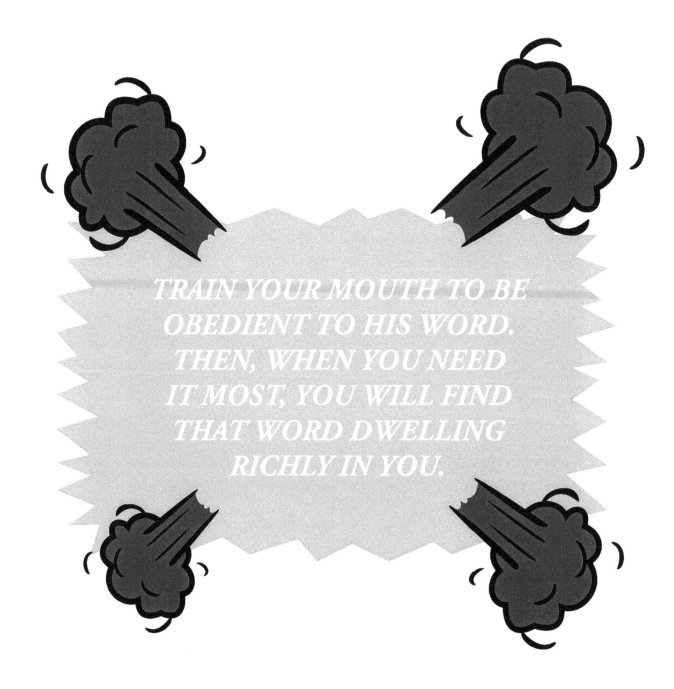

TRAIN YOUR MOUTH TO BE
OBEDIENT TO HIS WORD.
THEN, WHEN YOU NEED
IT MOST, YOU WILL FIND
THAT WORD DWELLING
RICHLY IN YOU.

*PROMISE TO HAVE
THE PATIENCE LOVE
DEMANDS AND
DESERVES.*

YOU CANNOT RECEIVE ALL OF WHAT GOD HAS FOR YOU IF YOU ARE NOT LIVING IN OBEDIENCE.

*A LESSON
TAUGHT IS
A LESSON
LEARNED.*

**EVERY DAY,
DO YOUR BEST,
AND GOD WILL
DO THE REST!**

YOUR GOAL
EVERY DAY SHOULD BE
TO ACT MORE LIKE
JESUS.

LORD, PLEASE HELP ME TO NEVER BE OVERWHELMED OR UNDERWHELMED BY ANYTHING THAT MAY OR MAY NOT BE HAPPENING IN MY LIFE BUT TO BE CONTENT IN WHATSOEVER STATE I AM IN!

SPEAK WHAT YOU SEEK UNTIL YOU SEE WHAT YOU'VE SAID. WHEN LIVING IN THE WORD OF GOD, YOUR HEART AND MOUTH MUST BE IN ALIGNMENT. SPEAK WHAT YOU FEEL, AND BELIEVE IT INTO EXISTENCE.

NOT EVERY PERSON
WILL THINK THE WAY
YOU DO. THEREFORE,
NEVER EXPECT THEM TO
DO THINGS THE WAY YOU
WOULD. ACCEPT THEM
FOR WHO AND WHAT
THEY ARE.

WHEN IT COMES
TO LOVE, LET IT LEAD
WITH YOUR HEART AND
NOT WITH YOUR MIND.

STOP THINKING SO MUCH. GET OUT OF YOUR HEAD. BE PRESENT, AND LIVE IN THE MOMENT.

WAIT, BE STILL, GET QUIET, BE PATIENT; IT WILL HAPPEN. DON'T DESPAIR OR GIVE UP HOPE. UNTIL THEN, STAY PRODUCTIVE, DEVELOP THE CHARACTERISTIC OF PATIENCE, AND LET NOTHING DISTURB YOU. PATIENCE IS THE COMPANION TO WISDOM.

NO ONE HAS THE POWER TO DO FOR ME WHAT ONLY GOD CAN.

NO WEAPON
FORMED AGAINST
YOU SHALL PROSPER.

THE POWER TO BELIEVE IS TO ENJOY WHAT IS AROUND YOU. TO BE CHEERFUL IS A GIFT TO GOD. IF YOU BELIEVE IN WHAT YOU ASK IN THE NAME OF GOD, HIS JOB WILL COME TO FRUITION, AND IT WILL MANIFEST.

THE POWER OF FAITH IS UNDENIABLE. IT CHANGES YOU AND EVERYTHING AROUND YOU. NEVER DEPART FROM YOUR TEACHINGS AND TRAINING.

SAY ALOUD:
I CAN DO ALL THINGS
THROUGH CHRIST WHO
STRENGTHENS ME!

HAVE A NATURAL CONFIDENCE ABOUT YOURSELF THAT FOLLOWS YOU WHEREVER YOU GO. IT'S NOT LOUD OR ABRASIVE OR ATTENTION-SEEKING BUT POSITIVE AND ENDEARING.

THE WAY YOU DO THINGS EXISTS IN THE SPACE BETWEEN EFFORT AND EASE. NEVER TRY TO FORCE THINGS THAT WON'T FIT OR BELIEVE IN LEAVING THINGS TO CHANCE. ALWAYS STRIKE SOMEWHERE IN THE MIDDLE.

KNOW THE DIFFERENCE
BETWEEN WANTING TO BE
LIKED BY EVERYONE AND
TREATING EVERYONE
WITH CLASS AND
RESPECT.

YOU ARE NO PUSHOVER, AND IF THE SITUATION CALLS FOR IT, BE UNAFRAID TO GIVE PEOPLE THE HARSH TRUTHS THEY MIGHT NOT WANT TO HEAR.

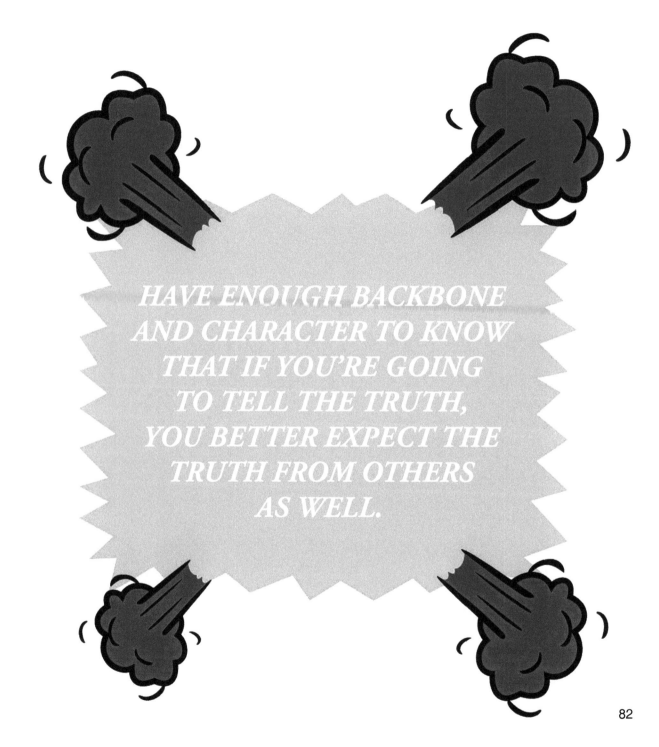

HAVE ENOUGH BACKBONE AND CHARACTER TO KNOW THAT IF YOU'RE GOING TO TELL THE TRUTH, YOU BETTER EXPECT THE TRUTH FROM OTHERS AS WELL.

82

YOU SHOULD KNOW THE DIFFERENCE BETWEEN POSITIVE CRITICISM AND NEGATIVE CRITICISM

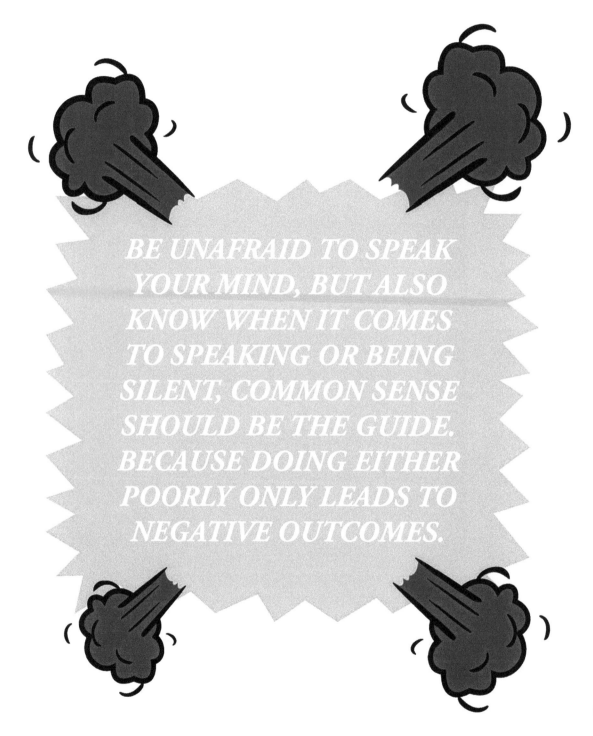

BE UNAFRAID TO SPEAK YOUR MIND, BUT ALSO KNOW WHEN IT COMES TO SPEAKING OR BEING SILENT, COMMON SENSE SHOULD BE THE GUIDE. BECAUSE DOING EITHER POORLY ONLY LEADS TO NEGATIVE OUTCOMES.

HAVE YOUR OWN SENSE OF STYLE. DON'T FEEL THE NEED TO BUY INTO SOCIETY'S SILLY EXPECTATIONS FOR WHAT YOU SHOULD WEAR, HOW YOU SHOULD LOOK, AND SO FORTH. BE YOUR OWN INDIVIDUAL, AND SET YOUR OWN FASHION LANE.

IT IS THE EASIEST THING IN THE WORLD TO JUDGE ANOTHER WOMAN AND MAKE COMPARISONS OUT OF INSECURITY. BE MINDFUL OF THIS, AND MAKE EVERY EFFORT NOT TO BE INTIMIDATED BY ANOTHER WOMAN'S BEAUTY, ACHIEVEMENT, OR SUCCESS BECAUSE YOU ARE JUST AS AMAZING. WE NEED TO UPLIFT, EMPOWER, AND STRENGTHEN ONE ANOTHER. WE ARE ALL JUST TRYING TO MAKE IT THROUGH THIS THING CALLED LIFE!

YOU DON'T HAVE
TO HAVE IT ALL
TOGETHER TO KEEP
MOVING FORWARD.
EMBRACING YOUR
LEGACY IS NOT THE
SAME AS HAVING
ALL THE ANSWERS.

KNOW HOW TO WALK AWAY FROM RELATIONSHIPS THAT ARE HARMFUL. NOT JUST ROMANTIC RELATIONSHIPS BUT FRIENDSHIPS, WORK CONTACTS, AND THE LIKE. ABUSE IS ABUSIVE, WHETHER MENTAL OR PHYSICAL.

DO NOT USE
PEOPLE FOR SELFISH
MOTIVATIONAL GAINS.
IN ANY AND ALL
RELATIONSHIPS, MAKE
SURE TO BELIEVE IN
RECIPROCITY, AND GIVE
WITHOUT EXPECTING
ANYTHING BACK.

SEEK A STRONG SUPPORT GROUP. KNOW EVERYONE NEEDS HELP, LOVE, AND STRENGTH, BUT ALSO KNOW EVERYONE MUST MENTALLY AND PHYSICALLY BELIEVE THEY ARE ENOUGH.

WHEN THERE IS A PROBLEM, PUT IT IN PERSPECTIVE. IS THIS A BIG PROBLEM, OR IS THIS A MINOR BUMP IN THE ROAD THAT YOU CANNOT MAKE A BIG DEAL AND JUST GET THROUGH?

*IT IS ALWAYS
BETTER TO ASK THAN
TO ASSUME. KNOW HOW
TO COMMUNICATE YOUR
NEEDS TO THOSE AROUND
YOU WITHOUT MAKING
ASSUMPTIONS.*

KNOW HOW TO COMMIT TO GETTING WHAT YOU WANT AND HOW TO BE SINGLE-MINDED ABOUT IT, BUT ALSO KNOW FAILURE IS A PART OF LIFE. DON'T LET IT KILL YOUR SPIRIT, BUT LET IT INVIGORATE YOU TO SEE OPPORTUNITIES OR GAIN A NEW PERSPECTIVE.

DEAL WITH YOUR EMOTIONS, AND PUT THEM INTO PERSPECTIVE. KNOW IT'S OKAY TO BE VULNERABLE AND WEAK. UNDERSTAND STRENGTH COMES FROM THESE PLACES. EVERYTHING YOU FEEL SHOULD BE ACKNOWLEDGED, EVEN WHEN IT DOESN'T NEED TO BE ACTED UPON.

LIFE IS ONE OF
THE MOST IMPORTANT
KEYS TO A SUCCESSFUL,
FULFILLING ONE. WHETHER
IT'S WORK OR PLAY,
IF YOU PUT EFFORT
INTO YOUR LIFE,
YOU WILL ALSO
ENJOY IT.

HUMAN CONNECTION COUNTS. PEOPLE WILL REMEMBER HOW YOU MAKE THEM FEEL, SO OPERATE WITH EMPATHY, PATIENCE, FOCUS, AND HUMILITY.

YOU CAN BE TOO WEIRD FOR ONE PLACE AND TOO NORMAL FOR A DIFFERENT PLACE. MAYBE WE CAN JUST FOCUS ON BEING OURSELVES, WHATEVER THAT MEANS AND HOWEVER THAT CHANGES.

FEELING BUMMED BY MIDDAY? BLOOD SUGAR IS KEY. IF YOU WANT TO BE YOUR BEST SELF—AND NOT THE CRABBY, SNAPPY, TOO-TIRED SELF THAT SOMETIMES MAKES AN APPEARANCE—EAT BREAKFAST, AND GET OUT OF YOUR SEAT.

IF YOU'RE NOT TAKING OWNERSHIP OF YOUR LIFE, SOMEONE ELSE WILL. NOW IS ALWAYS THE TIME TO TAKE CONTROL OF YOUR DECISIONS. IT'S ONLY IF YOU THINK "IT'S TOO LATE" THAT IT WILL BE.

BE PERSISTENT ABOUT PUTTING YOURSELF IN AWKWARD, UNCOMFORTABLE SITUATIONS AS OFTEN AS POSSIBLE. THAT'S WHEN YOUR BOX GETS A LITTLE BIGGER.

REJECTION IS NOT THE END-ALL-BE-ALL. LET THAT SLAP IN THE FACE SHAPE YOUR DREAM, AND DON'T RESIST THE SURPRISING NEW DIRECTION THAT SEEMS TO BE CALLING YOUR NAME.

DON'T BE AFRAID TO SHARE YOUR STORY. YOU DON'T KNOW WHERE IT COULD TAKE YOU OR WHO MIGHT NEED TO HEAR IT.

*DRESS TO GET
THE RIGHT KIND OF
ATTENTION. THE KIND
THAT HIGHLIGHTS WHO
YOU ARE INSIDE, WHAT
YOUR MIND IS CAPABLE
OF, AND THE AMAZING
THINGS YOU'RE DOING.*

POSITIVITY AND
PROBLEM SOLVING
WILL GET YOU
EVERYWHERE
YOU NEED TO GO.

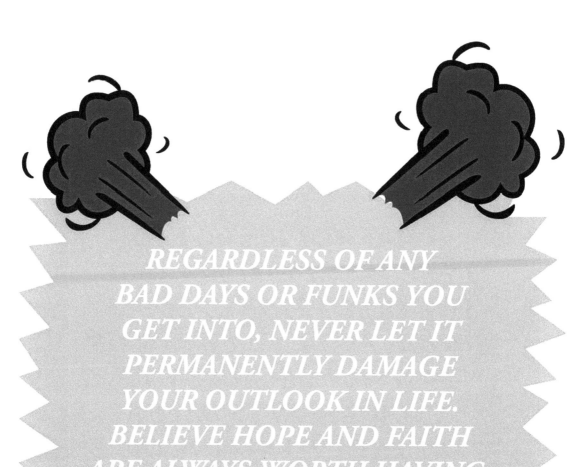

REGARDLESS OF ANY BAD DAYS OR FUNKS YOU GET INTO, NEVER LET IT PERMANENTLY DAMAGE YOUR OUTLOOK IN LIFE. BELIEVE HOPE AND FAITH ARE ALWAYS WORTH HAVING, AND TOMORROW CAN ALWAYS BE A BETTER DAY.

*NEVER DOUBT YOU
ARE VALUABLE AND
POWERFUL AND DESERVING
OF EVERY CHANCE AND
OPPORTUNITY IN THE
WORLD TO PURSUE
AND ACHIEVE YOUR
OWN DREAMS.*

*RAISE YOUR VOICE,
NOT TO SHOUT BUT SO
THOSE WITHOUT A VOICE
CAN BE HEARD. NOT EVERYONE
HAS THE POWER TO SPEAK
UP, BUT YOU CAN BE THEIR
STRENGTH. IT TOOK WOMEN
A LONG TIME TO DEVELOP
A VOICE, AND NOW THAT
YOU HAVE IT, DON'T
BE SILENT.*

IT ISN'T ABOUT MAKING WOMEN STRONG. WOMEN ARE ALREADY STRONG. IT'S ABOUT CHANGING THE WAY THE WORLD PERCEIVES OUR STRENGTH.

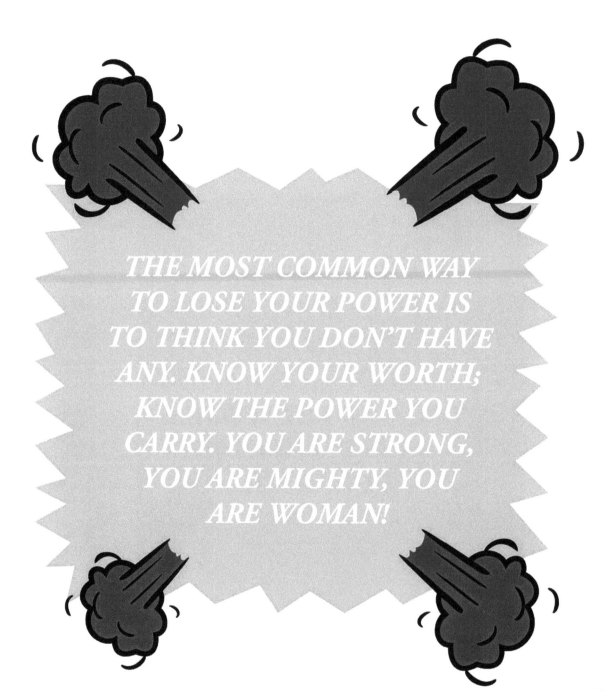

THE MOST COMMON WAY TO LOSE YOUR POWER IS TO THINK YOU DON'T HAVE ANY. KNOW YOUR WORTH; KNOW THE POWER YOU CARRY. YOU ARE STRONG, YOU ARE MIGHTY, YOU ARE WOMAN!

YOU ARE STRONG BECAUSE YOU KNOW YOUR WEAKNESSES. YOU ARE BEAUTIFUL BECAUSE YOU ARE AWARE OF YOUR FLAWS. YOU ARE FEARLESS BECAUSE YOU KNOW GOD HAS YOUR BACK. YOU ARE WISE BECAUSE YOU LEARN FROM YOUR MISTAKES. YOU KNOW LOVE BECAUSE YOU HAVE FELT HATE.

DO NOT BELIEVE IN REGRETS. NOT BECAUSE YOU DON'T THINK PEOPLE SHOULD LEARN FROM THEIR PAST BUT BECAUSE YOU KNOW REGRETS HAVE A TENDENCY TO KEEP PEOPLE CRIPPLED IN THEIR PAST, AND YOU DEFINITELY DON'T BELIEVE IN DOING THAT.

ABOUT THE AUTHOR

Adriana Clark-Rambert is a California native, born and raised in Los Angeles. Adriana, also known as Adriana Sheri, started her career as a runway and fashion model. She continued her journey as a young business mogul, working with high-profile entertainers in establishing their empires and helping their dreams come to fruition. Although it was a blessing, it was also time for her to build and flush out her own. She continues her journey, pursuing her passion as a fresh new-faced actress, while simultaneously building her first calling . . . to serve others. Adriana is a philanthropist at heart with her own organization called Godiss Love. She is very well-versed and a respected businesswoman with beauty, brains, and heart.